Biscuit's Valentine's Day

story by ALYSSA SATIN CAPUCILLI
pictures by PAT SCHORIES

HarperFestival®
A Division of HarperCollinsPublishers

"I'm almost finished making our valentines, Biscuit,"
said the little girl.
"And just in time! Today is Valentine's Day!"

Woof, woof!

"Are you ready to deliver our valentines, Biscuit?"

Woof!

"Wait for me, Biscuit!"
Woof, woof!

"Here's Daisy!"
Woof, woof!

"Funny puppy!
You have some special
valentines to
deliver, too."

Meow!

"Is Puddles home?"

Woof, woof!

"Special delivery from Biscuit!
Happy Valentine's Day, Daisy!"

"Happy Valentine's Day, Puddles!"

Bow wow!

"Let's see if Grandma and Grandpa are home."

Woof, woof!

"Silly puppy, these cookies aren't for you!
Happy Valentine's Day!"

"Let's hurry home and check our mailbox, Biscuit."

Woof!

"Look, Biscuit! Valentines for both of us!"

Woof, woof!

"Biscuit, where did you go? There's one more!

"Sweet puppy, I love you!
Happy Valentine's Day, Biscuit!"

I made a special valentine for you."

Woof, woof!